Messy Molly

Jo Williamson

D0549387

I2718150

For Nick

First published in 2016 by Scholastic Children's Books
Euston House, 24 Eversholt Street
London NW1 1DB
a division of Scholastic Ltd
www.scholastic.co.uk
London ~ New York ~ Toronto ~ Sydney ~ Auckland
Mexico City ~ New Delhi ~ Hong Kong

Text and Illustrations copyright © 2016 Jo Williamson

HB ISBN 978 - 1407 - 15277 - 6
PB ISBN 978 - 1407 - 15278 - 3

All rights reserved
Printed in Malaysia

1 3 5 7 9 10 8 6 4 2

The moral rights of Jo Williamson have been asserted.

Papers used by Scholastic Children's Books are made from wood grown in sustainable forests.

SCHOLASTIC

Molly starts each day looking lovely and clean . . .

Molly's
dog Pip

. . . but it never ever lasts.

This week, Molly decides to practise staying neat and tidy because she is singing in the school show on Saturday . . . in a lovely new white dress.

No spaghetti for you Pip –
you'll get it everywhere.

On Monday, it rained.

Luckily I have my umbrella.

The rain had stopped on Tuesday . . .

. . . so dodging the puddles on her scooter was a fun way for Molly to get to school.

I'm sure the teacher won't notice a bit of mud.

On Wednesday, Molly tried to bake some cakes,
wearing her apron to keep her dress spick and span.

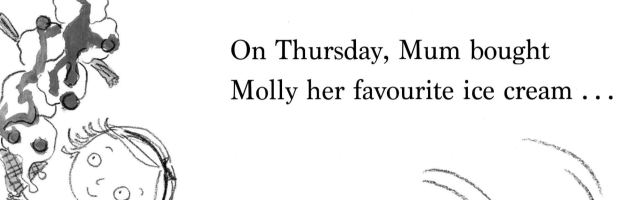

On Thursday, Mum bought
Molly her favourite ice cream . . .

. . . the TRIPLE double-decker
with cherries and a dollop
of raspberry sauce.

Ooh, triple trouble!

Molly's only mistake on Friday . . .

. . . was not wearing her GREEN dress.

Come on Pip,
let's go home.

And now Saturday was here.
Molly loved her dress . . .

. . . and would try very VERY hard not to get messy.

Ok Pip, you can come but we are not going to the park.

Molly thought it was safer to leave the troublesome
scooter at home and walk to school.

An ice cream would be nice . . . but maybe not today.

She noticed the puddles . . .
just in time.

Molly was nearly
at school now, but . . .

WET
PAINT

. . . WATCH OUT!

Phew! That was close.

Molly had made it!

She was SO proud that she had managed to keep tip-top tidy.

Well . . . ALMOST!